THE EMPIRE STRIKES BACK™

LONDON, NEW YORK, MUNICH,
MELBOURNE, AND DELHI

Editor Emma Grange
Designer Jon Hall
Senior Pre-Production Producer Jennifer Murray
Producer Louise Minihane
Managing Editor Elizabeth Dowsett
Design Manager Ron Stobbart
Publishing Manager Julie Ferris
Art Director Lisa Lanzarini
Publishing Director Simon Beecroft

Designed for DK by Sandra Perry

Reading Consultant
Maureen Fernandes

Dorling Kindersley would like to thank: Randi Sørensen and
Robert Stefan Ekblom at the LEGO Group and J. W. Rinzler,
Leland Chee, Troy Alders and Carol Roeder at Lucasfilm.

First published in Great Britain in 2014 by
Dorling Kindersley Limited
80 Strand, London, WC2R 0RL

10 9 8 7 6 5 4 3 2 1
001–196542–July/14

Page design copyright © 2014 Dorling Kindersley Limited

A CIP catalogue record for this book
is available from the British Library.

ISBN: 978-1-40934-969-3

Colour reproduction in the UK by Altaimage
Printed and bound in China

Discover more at
www.dk.com
www.starwars.com
www.LEGO.com/starwars

Contents

LEGO STAR WARS™

THE EMPIRE STRIKES BACK™

Written by
Emma Grange

An evil Empire

The Emperor is angry.

He has taken over the galaxy, but some rebels are trying to stop him.

Darth Vader   Darth Sidious

The Emperor is an evil Sith Lord called Darth Sidious. He has an apprentice called Darth Vader.

Darth Sidious tells Darth Vader that the rebels must be found and destroyed.

Darth Vader obeys his Master. He sends probe droids to search the galaxy for the rebels.

The Sith
The evil Sith seek power for themselves. There are only two Sith at one time: a Master and an apprentice.

The rebels

Here are the rebels.
They are hiding in a far
corner of the galaxy on
a planet called Hoth.

Hoth

Han Solo   Luke Skywalker   Princess Leia

Luke Skywalker is a very special rebel. His father was once a famous Jedi. Now Luke wants to become a Jedi, too.

Luke has many friends among the rebels. They are all prepared to fight the Empire.

Jedi Skywalker
The Jedi fight to protect the galaxy from evil forces. Luke is one of the last Jedi left in the galaxy.

Rebel base

The galaxy is full of many kinds of planets. Hoth is a cold place, covered in snow and ice. Nobody lives here, which makes it an excellent place to hide.

The rebels have built a secret base. Here it is, hidden in the snow.

The rebels are planning an attack on the Empire.

They need to hurry, because
Darth Vader's probe droids
are on their way!

Probe Droid
Probe droids are
programmed to search
for people and objects
without being spotted.

Princess Leia

Chewbacca

Wampa attack

There are dangerous creatures lurking in Hoth's snowdrifts. This hairy beast with sharp claws and horns is a wampa.

It has captured Luke and taken him back to its cave. Wampas are carnivores and like to eat people. Look out, Luke!

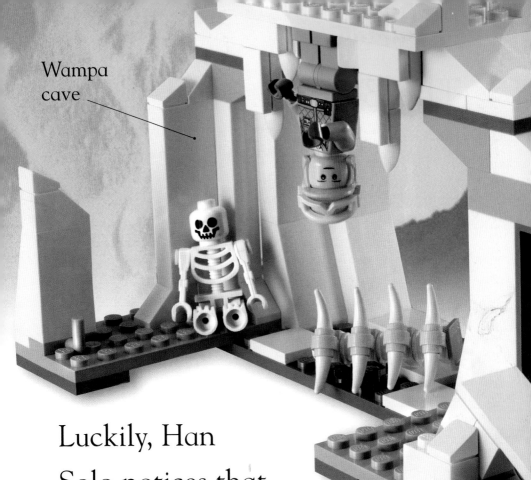

Wampa
cave

Luckily, Han
Solo notices that
Luke is missing and
rushes to rescue him.

Bacta Tank
After freezing in the cold,
Luke undergoes medical
treatment in a bacta
tank. The tank contains
special healing liquid.

The Battle of Hoth

Nothing stays a secret from the Empire for long. Darth Vader's probe droids have discovered the rebels on Hoth.

The Sith Lord sends an army to Hoth to destroy the base.

Giant AT-AT walkers march across the snow, firing at the rebels. They trample anything that gets in their way.

Snowspeeder

Rebel pilots try to bring down the AT-ATs with their agile snowspeeders, but the enemy vehicles are too powerful.

AT-AT walker

Brave rebels

Luke has a cunning plan.
He climbs up one of the AT-ATs
and destroys it from the inside!

*Millennium
Falcon*

The rebels fight the Empire's army bravely, but they are not able to stop the Empire from blowing up their base on Hoth.

Just in time, Han Solo escapes with Princess Leia in his ship, the *Millennium Falcon*, while Luke zooms off in his X-wing. Where will they go now?

X-wing

Jedi training

Who is this green creature?

On the dark and swampy
planet of Dagobah, Luke has
found Yoda, the greatest Jedi
Master of all time. Now Luke
can begin his Jedi training.

Yoda may be small and
old, but he is wise and
strong. He teaches Luke
to control the Force and
resist the dark side.

The Sith use the dark side of
the Force for evil, but the Jedi
believe in using their powers
only for good.

The Force
The Force is a powerful
energy used by the
Jedi and the Sith.
Yoda uses it to lift Luke's
X-wing out of the swamp!

Bounty hunters

Darth Vader is determined
to capture Luke Skywalker.
He knows that the young Jedi is
powerful and wants him stopped.

Dengar

IG-88

These suspicious looking
criminals are bounty hunters.

Bounty hunters will work for
anyone who will pay them a high
price. They specialise in hunting
down and capturing people.
Darth Vader wants them to
capture Luke and his friends!

Boba Fett

Bossk

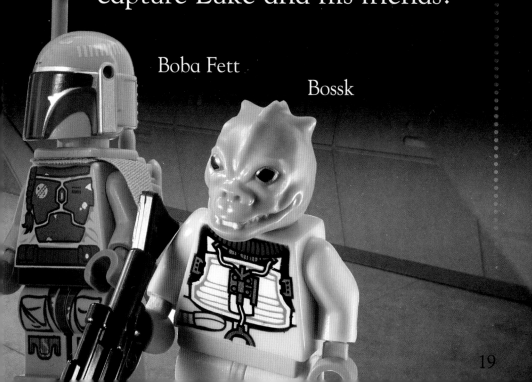

Boba Fett

This bounty hunter is
Boba Fett. He has been
promised a large reward
if he captures Han Solo.

rangefinder

Slave I

Boba Fett has a ship called
Slave I. He uses his tracking
skills to follow Han Solo's
Millennium Falcon.

Cloud City

Han Solo and Princess Leia
flee to Cloud City. This city
floats high among the clouds,
and is ruled by Lando Calrissian,
an old friend of Han's.

Lando
Calrissian

Lando used to be a smuggler.
Can he be trusted to help Han?

Lando doesn't tell Han that
Boba Fett followed them all the
way to Cloud City. Darth Vader
is now waiting for them. Uh-oh!

Trapped!
Darth Vader's fierce
stormtroopers
surround the rebels.
It looks like there
is no way out!

Shocking truth

Through the power of the Force, Luke senses that his friends are in trouble. But he arrives too late – and comes face to face with Darth Vader!

Luke puts his new Jedi skills to the test as he duels the evil Sith Lord.

Darth Vader tries to convince
Luke to join the dark side.
Finally, he reveals the truth:
Darth Vader is Luke's father!

Friends to the rescue

What will happen to the
rebels next? Han Solo has been
captured by Boba Fett. Despite
fighting bravely, Luke has been
injured by Darth Vader.

Lando Calrissian is sorry that
he couldn't stop Han from being
captured. He manages to escape
Cloud City with Princess Leia.
As they leave, they also manage
to rescue Luke.

Dark times

As Darth Vader returns to
the Emperor, it looks like the
Empire is stronger than ever.

The rebels have suffered
several defeats.

Some of them, like Han Solo, have been captured, but his loyal friends are flying off to rescue him.

The rebels won't give up hope just yet!

Quiz

1. What planet were the rebels hiding on?

2. What type of droid is this?

3. What is this person's job?

4. What is Boba Fett's ship called?

5. Who does Luke Skywalker find on the planet Dagobah?

1. Hoth 2. Probe droid 3. Bounty hunter 4. *Slave 1* 5. Yoda

30

Index

Here are some other DK books you might enjoy.

LEGO® *Star Wars*™ The Phantom Menace™
Who has brought the LEGO® *Star Wars*™ galaxy
to the brink of war? Can the Jedi stop them?

LEGO® *Star Wars*™ Attack of the Clones™
Meet evil Count Dooku! Can the Republic's
clone troopers defeat the Sith's droid army?

Angry Birds™ *Star Wars*™ **Path to the Pork Side**
Can Redkin Skywalker resist the power of the
Pork Side? Join the young Jedi Bird on his journey!

LEGO® *Star Wars*™ Revenge of the Sith™
The Jedi must save the galaxy from the Sith!
Will Anakin fall to the dark side?

LEGO® *Star Wars*™ Return of the Jedi™
Luke Skywalker is the last Jedi in the galaxy.
Can he help the rebels defeat the evil Empire?

LEGO® Legends of Chima™**: Race for CHI**
Jump into battle with the animal tribes as
they fight to get their claws on the CHI!